Paradise Enclave

By Alexandria Venture

Copyright 2023

Introduction

A tropical and erotic horror exists on a mysterious island. It looks so peaceful; a place to escape from turmoil. But who or what lives inside? Some places were never meant to be disturbed. The island of Yupa contains many strange secrets...

This erotica is for those eager to see action in every chapter. The author does not believe in too much teasing. This unique and intense fantasy story will take you on an adventure you've not seen yet before or even fathomed.

Contents: Mdom, coercion, M/F, bondage, oviposition, virginity, sleep sex, Fpreg, inflation, creature, incubation, harem, experiments, vaginal, anal, oral, captors, alien, genetic modification.

This is a work of fiction. Any names or characters, businesses or places, events or incidents, are fictitious. Any resemblance to actual persons, living or dead, or actual events is purely coincidental.

The illustrations in this book are purely from royalty-free open-source artificial intelligence programs.

Table of Contents

1

Travelling with Treasure

The angry sea tossed as though it was fighting a battle to the death. Its waves threw powerful blows to the sides of the impressive wooden ship. All that were on the ship had gone downstairs to remain safe from the storm. The captain drew up the sails as not to be pushed over into the sea. The storm remained for hours.

Fifty-three young women huddled together downstairs. The captain was the only male on the ship. They had free reign of the ship; although their captor ensured they had no way to escape the trip. He was kind to them, however. There was never a reason for violence or pressure. They were simply being transported from one continent to another. It was for their own benefit, as the region they were from was being overtaken in a war. The young girls were thankful for being alive.

Each of the women were adults; albeit young adults. Some of them had never yet been in a relationship before. Others had, but none of them had married yet. They were chosen as prime of the crop, with intent of being valuable assets on a new land. But, none of them could predict what the weather had in store for them.

The captain's name was Captain Hunter Totem. He carried himself proudly, but not in a disrespectful manner. Hunter knew his own limits well. Every action he took was for his own benefit, but not so much to put others down. While he could be perceived as haughty from the outside, he was actually kind and just. His mission was always clear in his own mind.

All of the women on the ship respected him. It was a difficult choice to have to pluck them from the scene of the war and leave everything behind. He had lost his entire family as well as them. Their only chance was to start anew. Each day got better during their travels at first. The fishing was plenty, and he had a contraption that filtered seawater into drinking water. They had everything they needed and then some. The ship was a safe place to be in general, and it was welcomed as a break from the war.

After the pain of the past began to fade over a month or so, the females began to calm. They made friends with each other, and the captain as well. It wasn't long before they noticed some of his more prominent features, such as his muscular build and attractive shaven beard. It was a short beard but it maintained his manliness. As they joked with him, he could cackle in shared return. But he had no intent of getting involved with them on the trip to their destination. Such an act would complicate his mission, of course.

On one hot day, Captain Totem was stretched out on one of his chairs as he took in the sun. He was on the verge of falling asleep; when he heard a couple girls giggling in the bathhouse. He cracked one eye open just in time to see two of them rushing from one room to another. Just smelling female on them was torturous for him, but he maintained his composure most of the time. There were some occasions that his sea serpent was more than eager to grow in readiness. Viewing the two running across the hall with their shapely naked bodies was enough to put him on edge. His erection was seen to everyone for half of the day, and was so tight against his pants that everyone could see the definition of the penis head and the length of the shaft going almost to his knee.

He often wondered how many of them were actually virgins. When he rescued them, they were grouped together in a sanctuary. His duty was to guide them out and onto his ship into safety. Many of them had just reached adulthood. He imagined that many of them had probably never been meddled with before, as they had just recently reached adulthood. Their shyness was also a telltale sign. He could smell their fertility on them. They were ready to breed. But the time wasn't right. Not yet.

As the storm thrashed into the side of the ship, it busted open a couple planks on her left. Water rushed into the hull. The women quickly ran up to the deck. Now, it was only a matter of time. The ship was no longer a safe place to be; they thought. An hour of water seeping into the hull had the ship leaning to one side slightly. The waves sloshed into the ship continuously, and everyone was separated in the horrific storm.

After the entire night of the terrifying storm, the seas finally calmed. The ship managed to maintain itself upright, despite being crooked. The captain had lost complete track of where they were. Even if he knew, there would be no way of guiding the ship in the condition it was now in.

It took a day for everyone on the ship to settle down. They were focused on gathering food and water supplies that had been strewn about, organizing broken items or tossing trash off the ship. After a while, the females sat down together to catch up and discuss their survival as well as their future ahead.

Captain Totem was now certain they had to be doomed. Their food supplies might last them a couple weeks, maximum. After that, starvation would begin. His usual fishing equipment had been completely damaged from the storm. They were just lucky enough that the ship was still floating.

He approached the group of broads. "Looks like we've found ourselves in a predicament". He said plainly. Half of the women scowled, as he stated the obvious. Most of them were fearful of what was to come. Death would be a likely possibility at this point. "What do we do now?" Rosina piped in. She had red hair and blue eyes. "We go where the sea has the mercy to take us." He replied. "There's no telling where we are on the map. My instruments are damaged." She looked back down in disappointment.

As the evening set, Captain Totem began to ponder. His precious cargo would certainly never be delivered to its destination now. They may all have to starve to death on this ship. What else could be done? He stared out into the sunset. The ship was full of beautiful, still healthy women. They were now effectively his. Women have their own needs, whether they admit it or not. Perhaps it was his task to help them along.

His heavy scrotum was so full and tight. It was agonizing to have to hold it any longer. Withdrawing again, he took his wide rod in hand and began stroking it frantically. Her juices lubricated him perfectly for this.

At just the right moment, he plugged his penis head right back into her halfway, sealing her tight hole. Thick strands of hot white cum shot deep into her. Every shot of cum pooled into a thick potent gush of serum into her. He stayed in this position for perhaps a half hour. This would increase chances of pregnancy. Her staying in a laying down position would also help that possibility. But he wasn't in very far when he came. The fertilization would remain a mystery for now.

He left the room, very well spent. The others just assumed he went in there smooching on her. When the girl finally awoke, she noticed a soreness of her hole. It felt like it had been well used, but it's not like her virginity had been taken. It had been several hours since the encounter. She got up slowly to use the bathroom, and sat down on the toilet. As she began to urinate, white globs of semen dropped from her. She wasn't sure what it was. She didn't feel ill, so at least she didn't have a sickness to worry about. Her fantasies went wild for the next few days. She would love to mate with the captain. But such a wish would probably sound ridiculous to him, she thought.

For the next few days, everyone ate canned meat and vegetables. The fresh fish had all been eaten. Their bones were dried out and preserved for later use, because they contained nutrients. The overall morale on the ship decreased daily. Their fate approached quickly.

The captain wondered if Rosina had any clue of what happened. He emptied his balls into her that night. Surely, she would notice the thick load seeping out of her. But would she expect that to have happened? Probably not. He thought of monitoring her, but the thought passed quickly as he feared of everyone's demise on the ship. It wouldn't matter if she had become fertilized by him or not. They were bound to all die within a month or two. At least, their water filtration system was still in operation. That would keep them alive for a decent amount of time.

Sandra stared at Rosina. She knew that was the girl that had been 'smooching' with the captain the other night. She didn't want to admit it, but Sandra was jealous. They had been 'kissing' for quite a while that night, and anything could have happened. Captain Totem was severely handsome. Any female would do anything to carry his offspring, she thought. Seeing the circumstances, Sandra walked right up to Rosina and blatantly asked the question. "Is Totem a good kisser?" Rosina blushed at the question, despite being innocent. "I wouldn't know". She looked away. Sandra wasn't satisfied with her answer, but let her be after that. Perhaps she needed to pursue him herself.

The next morning, the captain had managed to rig a fishing line up with some bait. He used a pulley to help himself pull up a decent sized fish. It was a large mahi mahi. All the crew clapped and cheered in unison. This meant they could survive a little while longer. Within minutes, he went into the kitchen to begin preparing the fish.

Upon entering the kitchen, Sandra's nostrils were immediately filled with the smell of fresh fish. Captain Totem was gutting it out and scaling it. He had done this his entire life, so it came natural to him. A couple other girls were there watching him work. None of them had noticed Sandra's entry.

The steel countertops wrapped around the entire kitchen. One of them branched into the kitchen midway. This is where the captain was working. Sandra started to crawl under the counter on the lower shelf. She had a plan. After a minute, she migrated underneath where he was working. The other females were not able to see her on the other side of the counter, due to boxes of storage on the other side.

His groin was right in Sandra's face. Every move made it obvious how large his member was. She was starving for it, as she was currently ovulating. Her natural desires controlled her now. To avoid startling him, she gently placed her hand over his groin. His conversation with the other girls stopped short. But after discovering what was happening, he continued his chatting with them. She rubbed her hand over his meat vertically. Without hesitation, she took her hands on either side of his shorts and pulled them down gently. Just enough to reveal a full view of what was inside.

His penis twitched and danced like a pony as it became visible. Sandra placed her nose directly under his member, nudging it up to rest on her face while she tugged on his taught sack with her teeth gently. He quickly became erect. At this moment, Sandra knew she could get what she wanted. The captain suddenly asked all the other girls to leave the room. He said, he had some private business to take care of here. They were confused, but followed orders promptly.

Sandra ran her tongue across the tip of his penis head. She playfully tried to fit her tongue tip inside his dick hole, but it was too small. Precum dripped onto her breast while she licked all over his shaft. After the girls left, he immediately dragged Sandra out from under the counter. He pushed her firmly face down into the floor, and picked up her rear so that she was on her knees with her ass facing the ceiling.

He took his fleshy uncircumcised rod and rubbed it up and down her slit. His own precum added lubrication; as if she needed more. He prodded her slightly. She was not a virgin, but she had not taken one his size before. The lubrication allowed him to pop his entire head in with ease. Her tight passage clung to his rod. He enjoyed her unique ridges as he began to hump into her wet cavern. The slapping noises were light at first. Her own fluids began to drip down from her vagina as he fucked her. There was no turning back now.

He gripped her hips and slammed hard into her once. She shrieked in pain, but wanted more. Almost his entire length was inside her. He had about three more inches to go. His eager cock twitched inside of her, starting to curve upward in further excitement. With one motion, he stabbed the remainder of his thick shaft into her. He was balls deep now. She yelped loudly. Surely, others have heard. But it didn't matter anymore. One spurt of cum sneaked out of his penis. His balls shuttered.

He withdrew again fully. Her hole was wider than before. She was now defiled by his monster cock. Sandra belonged to the captain now. He jabbed his thick meat back into her, one stroke at a time. Each thrust had him pulling all the way out again. His thrusts became violent now. She started to get a red spot where his heavy balls were slapping her ass. It stung her cheeks after each quick thrust. Sandra opened her legs a little more. This was enough to put him on edge. She wanted to get pregnant. He stabbed his pointed rod into her several more times with immense force, and then rammed into her once more to the hilt. He was balls deep in her. His powerful arms clenched her body into place. He cried out as he inseminated her, and she moaned loudly as well. His balls shrunk up for each injection, and fell dangling each time. Four spurts filled her up and emptied his balls yet again.

This would certainly be a successful mating. His insatiable lust was satisfied at least for now. He slapped Sandra on the ass as his soggy cock hung from his loins. She was immediately sore from the size of his dick. Captain Totem looked on the counter and grabbed three corks from wine bottles that were left over. He stuffed them into her breeding hole. "Go lay down and leave these in for a while. We don't want to waste my precious semen." She nodded, and limped off to the bedding area. In a way, he was proud of himself. He gained a harem incidentally, and they were probably becoming pregnant one by one. His instinct made him ignore the danger of survival they faced.

The other girls all knew what had happened. Sandra had been bred by the captain. It turned them on, but most of them couldn't yet bring themselves to admit such a thing. It was shrugged off and they continued to do their daily tasks without dwelling on it too much.

Each day that passed saw a decrease in morale on the hopeless ship. The canned goods were now very few. Of course, cannibalism was out of the question. The captain was able to catch a fish here and there with his line, but it wouldn't be near enough.

Another night approached quickly. The captain laid out on the bench belly down. The fertile women had watched him for quite a while. Surely it would be foolish to reproduce while survival was at stake. But what if he could provide nutrition in another way?

He had a towel over him as he slept. One of the girls in particular had been getting mere scraps of the meals, if that. She was beginning to starve. Her name was Tonya. She had black hair, a tan on her skin and light brown eyes. An idea popped into her head. While nobody else was looking, she crawled underneath his bench. The large towel concealed her. As she crawled, she felt something dragging across her back. She then spun her body around to lay on he back. Could it be? His entire package was hanging down through a slot in the bench.

There was enough moonlight to get a good look at it. His balls were rather round, but clearly heavy. The skin stretched to carry the weight of them. There was very little hair, if any. His penis wasn't erect as he was asleep. However, it was clearly an impressive sight despite this. His penis tip peeked out from his protective foreskin cover. The girth was something to behold. When it was erect, it had to be as thick as her arm if not more.

She breathed warm air on his hanging cock. It twitched lightly once. She then flicked her tongue down across the tip. The cock jerked upward once, then fell again. She looked to her left, and noticed a small bucket. In order to get the nutrition she needed, she would have to milk him like a cow.

She sucked on his tip for several minutes until precum started to drain out. She then used that as lubrication to wrap her hands around his shaft. It soon became very erect. She massaged his entire length and sucked on him until he came into the bucket. It sloshed into the bucket with immense force. But she wasn't done yet. Her speed quickened, and she flicked his dick tip violently with her tongue. He was on the verge of orgasming again, but withheld abruptly. He got up, picked her up from the ground and briskly carried her to his bedroom with a gigantic erection.

He placed her belly down onto his bed. She instinctually undressed. His hands guided her movements, and he spread her legs apart further. The room was lit with an oil candle. He got down on his knees to spread her cheeks apart and view her treasures. Her vagina hole was quite small. He wondered if he would even be able to fit his throbbing beast inside her.

The captain's cock had prominent veins pulsing on the sides of his penis. He still had cum on the tip. He took his warm shaft in his left hand and started rubbing the rigid yet soft mushroom head up and down her slit. She vibrated with excitement. Each time he went up and down the slit, he prodded her fertile hole with his cock head. She was ready to be bred.

He leaned his entire body over her deliberately. Then, when his cock was in a vertical position aimed into her opening, he fell on her with all of his weight into the bed. She cried out in pain and pleasure. Her body was filled tightly to the hilt with his organ. She was now a puppet to his desires. Her skewered body went limp as she now belonged to him.

He withdrew slightly, which triggered her orgasm. Her passage tugged and squeezed on his dick. She then struggled a little. Each movement she made was more pleasure for his rod.

He withdrew completely this time, and she gasped. He fell back onto her again, yet again stabbing into her with his thick member. Her opening was so tight at the base of his penis. One spurt of cum spilled out deep into her. He jabbed her twice more. Then, he was in a breeding rampage. He grabbed her waist and jackhammered her. The room echoed with the sound of his penis thrashing her cervix. He humped her for another 10 minutes. It seemed like hours to her.

He finally spewed out his last load. She was so full of semen and cock, that she had forgotten about her hunger. Little did she know, the other girls had devoured her bucket spoils in the meantime. He slowly withdrew his huge cock. It dropped down as it exited, dripping heavily. Her hole was completely defiled now. It appeared like it was trying to breathe. The opening gaped out more with every breath she took.

She put her hand on her belly. There was a painful round lump where his cum deposit bulged her insides and distended her stomach. A river of cum was getting ready to spill out, and he noticed. He quickly gathered some sheets, and propped up her bottom. "Stay in this position the rest of the night. We don't want my offspring to go to waste." She did as she was told, and even orgasmed on her own a couple times that night. This helped as her body sucked in the semen deeper into her body each time. There was no escaping her pregnancy now.

2

Survival

The only food now available was dried fish bones. The girls crunched on them whenever they got hungry. They all stared longingly off into the distance for hope. The ones acquainted with the captain tended to stay close to him. Rosina usually didn't move too far from him either. "How will be know if we're pregnant?" Sandra asked out loud. He smirked to himself. "Your little bellies will start to feel very tight. They'll get bigger and bigger. Then, your breasts will swell up with milk." She nodded in return.

Rosina looked upward into the sky. Something they hadn't seen on the trip since they started the voyage. Seagulls! The captain stood up suddenly. This was a sign of nearby land. He ran to the bow of the ship and looked out and pointed. It's land!! The entire crew cheered.

The ship could not be directed into any specific direction. They had no choice but to jump into the water and swim to the shore. It was about 200 yards away. Nobody stayed on the boat. They were all very eager to feel sand on their feet.

After some time passed, it seemed that everyone made it to shore. It was a tiresome workout. Most of the women seemed to meander away from the captain and go off on their own. It was unknown what their plan for survival was, but nobody could make them stay. The rest of them worked together to build shelter and clothing materials for themselves.

The island itself was quite warm and sunny. The white sand was hot to the touch. The cool wind whipped intermittently. Vegetation grew healthily and thick. Small hermit crabs fled at the sight of humans. Something was so pure about it. Despite this, it gave them an uneasy feeling; which they ignored.

The gracious island provided coconuts to eat and drink out of. This was a nice change for everyone. After another couple of weeks, they were decently established on the island for what they had to deal with. In the meantime, Captain Totem was working on building his relationship with Rosina. He imagined, her soreness would have gone away by now and healed back to its former state. Something about her in particular drove him to continue his pursuit with her.

"How are you feeling?" The captain asked Rosina at the campfire. It was well into the night. "Pretty good." She replied simply. She was too shy to confess her feelings to him. The other girls were sound asleep on the sand around them. "I'll go get some more fronds to burn on the fire." She walked off. He waited for one moment, and then followed.

It wasn't long before he found her plucking fronds in the moonlight. The light made her small figure shine. She had to be a mere 100 pounds. Quite a size difference from the captain, who was pushing about 185 pounds. He was almost twice her size, and all muscle. "I came to help", he said. She nodded and bent over one more time to grab another frond. He put his hand firmly on her shoulder and stood behind her, locking her in position. She gasped, but didn't resist.

He grinded his equipment on her small bottom; rolling everything back and forth over her buttocks. She became wet immediately. He could smell it on her, and peeled off her bottoms slowly. This was the same virgin he prodded earlier. He took his finger and slid it down her slit from the front, stopping to wiggle around her opening. Yes, she had definitely healed back well into virginity.

His cock twitched in anticipation. This would be no easy task. He pulled down his own pants as well, and let his cock lay on her back. It almost laid across the entire length of her small body. His heartbeat pulsed into the penis and she felt it on her. She started to drip in wetness. Totem pulled himself back, and slid his cock tip up and down her slit all the way. His length stimulated her as he carefully air-humped across her tender skin.

He then pointed the blunt head at her microscopic hole. At it's widest part, it was about two and a half inches wide when fully erect. He nudged it toward his goal. Her opening gave a little, but could hardly budge. Totem had her position herself in front of a palm tree for support. He pushed again. His eager penis head could just hardly peek inside.

Rosina got down on her knees and planted the side of her face onto the ground. This was going to require a bit of force. The cock tip began peeking in and out, but only halfway like last time. Each removal again made a loud suction noise. She then realized what had happened to her earlier, but welcomed the thought. Suddenly, all of his muscles became stiff. He had his dick head wedged halfway in her as he placed both of his hands on her shoulders. His balls bounced around as he began to prod her with quick, short humps.

In one motion, he shoved his entire cock head into her tight hole. Rosina yelped out in pain. Her hole clasped his sheath right behind the head. His entire cockhead was wrapped in tight, wet warmth. Totem was breathing quite heavy at this point. He had never penetrated a girl so small before. Her little legs quivered involuntarily. She had been invaded by an almost unnaturally shaped and sized object. His jizz leaked into her in satisfaction.

Totem attempted to withdraw, so he could repeat the process. When he pulled back, so did her entire body. They were stuck together like breeding dogs. She whimpered each time he tried to pull out. This excited him further. His dick tip spurted its sauce into her some but he was trying to withhold his final climax. Then, he stood up. She was forced onto her feet due to their connection. Finally, she held onto a tree and he stepped backward. The suction noise it made was significant. Fluid dripped from both of them. "We're going to have to work on you some, eh?" She smiled nervously. Her breeding hole was a bit bigger now from the penetration. They curled up next to the campfire and slept for the rest of the night.

The next morning, the group decided to search deeper into the island. After all, the others were essentially missing. Rosina could hardly walk from the night before. Each of the girls had to abide by a rule. If they had been inseminated, they had to plug their hole with something as not to waste the cum and increase chance of contraception. The exception is when they had to use the restroom.

By the time the four had walked for 13 miles, they were completely exhausted. Something strange could be seen in the distance. It looked like a building. Could it be, civilization here? However, it had already become dawn. They would have to reserve the last walk for the next morning as it was still quite far away.

In the night, Sandra and Tonya started to rub themselves on the captain. Within minutes he had bred both of them yet again. They were all dripping with semen, but nothing was around them to plug their openings. They just had to sleep with their rears propped up through the night.

3

A New Prospect

The morning finally approached, and the group awakened to the sight of the lighted building. They kept it in their sight as they walked on. Birds of paradise became disturbed of their presence and flew off abruptly. A strange looking snake crossed their path, but slithered quickly away at the sight of them. It was full of bright colors.

The tired group finally approached the front door of the mysterious building. It was surprisingly clean and well kept. A video camera pointed straight at them from the roof's eve. Before they could knock, the door was opened by a man in a white lab coat. "Welcome to the island." He smiled at them. "Where are we?" Sandra stammered. "All will be explained in time." He said simply, and welcomed them inside. The temperature of the building was a perfect 73 degrees Fahrenheit.

"My name is William Bellows. You may call me whatever you like." His assistant came out and distributed clothes to them. "This is Carey. She aids me in various projects around the laboratory. Go ahead and get clean in the showers, and get into fresh clothes. I'll explain more afterward." They all got clean quickly. Each of them was too nervous to do anything other than what was instructed of them. There were too many unanswered questions.

Carey greeted them as they emerged back into the main room. She seated them on couches while William the scientist approached them. Tonya was seen staring at a large photograph framed on the wall. It was photo of a bunch of snakes tangled together. They were the same colors as the one they saw on the way here. "That's called a mating ball." William saw her curiosity. "It's one of the things I study here on this island."

William sat down in the room with them. "I know about your shipwreck. There is video surveillance all over this island. I know quite a bit about your group." He smirked. "You all are welcome to stay here. You'll be a great help to my research. Anything you need will be provided." "What about the other girls from the ship?" The captain interrupted. "Don't worry, they appear to be doing well. They are still roaming the island... but they appear to have grouped together in order to survive."

Carey stood up. "Let's show you all around the facility." William left in another direction. The first area they passed had several comfortable looking bedrooms. As they walked on, the rooms started to look more like laboratories. Rosina poked her head into one of the rooms. The walls had lighted images of ultrasound results. They looked like strange embryos, but she couldn't be sure. Machines were also in quite a few rooms, with unknown purpose. There was a large fluid tank in one of the rooms. It caught their attention, but nobody knew what fluid could possibly be held inside of it.

They were all stopped at the end of the hall. "No one is to go into this room without the company of me or William. This is a highly restricted area." She said in a tone as if to pique curiosity in them. The door was opened and it was colder in the room. The walls were made of block and it was rather dark. The center of the area had a light with chairs and a table. "We found this creature on the island. It is very dangerous, but we are studying it. Never get too close to the cage as it has extremely high aggression." They peered into the cage but could hardly make out anything in the darkness. His eyes glistened as he stared back at them and breathed heavily. Captain Totem stared back apprehensively.

The girls immediately retreated for the hall, and Carey followed behind them. "It's getting close to evening. Why don't you all pick your bedrooms and get some sleep for the night?" Everyone nodded and dispersed. They each picked a separate bedroom, as to not cause issues with their host. It didn't take them all long to fall into a deep sleep.

At around midnight, Carey went into Rosina's room. She woke her gently. "Come, we've got to move you into another room." It almost seemed as though her drowsiness was being used as an upper hand. She was brought into a lab room down the hall. Upon entering, the lights were blindingly bright. Carey guided her to one of three special 'beds' in the room. "Now, I need you to lay face down on this." Rosina crawled onto the strange looking bed. It had her supported around her waist area and shoulders, as well as her head.

Immediately after laying down on it, Carey asked her to relax. She obeyed. While the device was odd, it was still quite comfortable. A strap was placed around her waist and neck as if to hold her in place. Her arms hung down and were also secured to vertical bars that supported the bed. Finally, her legs were pushed apart and a metal bar was placed between them. It had straps on each end that attached to her legs. "This will help with the insertion." Carey explained. This made Rosina quite nervous. She had no idea what was going on. A cloth strap was also wrapped firmly but comfortably around her mouth.

Tonya and Sandra had a similar fate, but they were not quite strapped as tight. Rosina was a special patient, as she had not undergone as extensive 'insertion' as the others. Finally, Captain Totem was awoken and brought into a different lab room. Carey had him stand next to a counter with a scale on it. She cupped her hands together to support his balls, and placed them on the scale. "One and a third pounds." She said out loud. "We're going to have to make sure you drink plenty of water to maintain your state." His hefty dick twitched from her touch.

She quickly guided the stallion of a man into the room with the tied up females. Sandra was rubbing her belly. "It's starting to feel like it's tightening." Carey turned to the captain. "We had to set this up while you all were still half asleep. You all can rest now. But you will be confined to this room for a while. Your object is to ensure impregnation from these females. Our machines are on the opposite sides of the walls. They can detect pregnancy, fertility, and everything else." The captain nodded, almost excitedly.

The girls squirmed about, but couldn't move very much. They were tied pretty tightly to the confines of their special breeding beds. He ran his hand up and down Rosina's leg. She started breathing more heavily and her breasts bounced a little. He moved to the front of the bed and reached forward, massaging her tight breasts. He wondered if milk had already started to form in them yet, or whether she truly was even pregnant yet. His cock stood to attention and rested on top of her head. The grapefruit-sized balls rubbed warmly in front of her face. She was starting to get wet.

The captain returned to her rear area, and parted her vaginal lips gently with this powerful large fingers. The opening was still a little red from when his cock head prodded her last time. She started to shiver in anticipation. He grabbed his thick shaft and positioned his blunt tip into her opening. His waist slowly leaned into her, his aching cock head yearning for more. Her entrance was so tight that it pushed back his foreskin all the way. In one movement, he popped his cock head past her virginity again. It was a little easier this time. Her virginity collar locked onto the throat of his cock as he enjoyed her tight opening.

This time, when he withdrew, he didn't have to worry about her locking onto him. He pulled his cock head back out and the motion sucked precum right out of his hole. It was an amazing feeling. She whimpered and her breathing became quicker. His cock was now fully erect, arching upward like a man showing off his biceps.

Some of Rosina's natural juices started to flow, and she dripped slightly. He pressed his warm fleshy head against her familiar opening again. It felt more welcoming to him now. Her hole was slightly wider and extremely lubricated. Her legs being forced apart helped him reach new depths, and allowed for his unrestricted movements.

He pressed into her again, letting her vulva lips swallow his rock-hard member one inch at a time. The thick head popped into her again. She whimpered and squirmed at his every move. The veins looked prevalent on his shaft as his blood pressure rose. He humped two short jabs into her a couple inches further, then withdrew completely again. The suction noise echoed throughout the room, and a strand of his cum still connected them together. She yelped at the painful intrusion. His cock was huge compared to the size of her tiny body.

A third of his penis was well lubricated now. He wasn't about to let it go to waste. He used his dick as a paintbrush and wiped up and down her slit, spreading the white creamy juices on and in her as he prodded her as well. She would get impregnated tonight. He slipped his penis into her sore hole again. This time he presses further in. He was halfway inside her now. The aquarium in his sack was perhaps more excited than it's ever been.

Finally, he began to hump her rhythmically. Half of his length slid tightly into her with each stroke. His heavy package danced to and fro. Rosina clenched the chair as he bred her intently. The shape of his dick could be seen bulging out from her small belly. The tip was larger, showing how far his dick tip went with each hump. His muscles became tense, and he gripped her waist. He humped once more, and sharply. His cock head struck against her cervix. Thick, chunky semen flowed into her depths.

The hot flood inside her was being sealed off by his own shaft. He wasn't finished with her though. He needed to get all the way inside her. Balls deep. He jabbed his rigid cock against her walls again. She gasped out in orgasm. Her insides twitched and squeezed his cock, exciting him further. His balls were still heavy with offspring.

He withdrew fully yet again. His expression was extremely focused; almost angry. He grabbed her tightly and began to pound into her. His cock head was banging at her cervical door. Every other hump granted his cock head a quick view into her womb. Her cervix squeezed his fleshy head tightly with each stroke. Tighter than her own virginity.

Finally, he forced his huge penis head into her tiny cervical opening. His angry member proudly aimed directly into her womb and shot a powerful load of potent sperm straight into her. He was all the way in her. She coughed and gasped at the feeling. Her entrance was stretched where the base of his shaft rested. It had a 3-and-a-half-inch diameter. She would never be the same after being bred by him.

Her womb became tight and full of his hot cum. Her hanging belly looked pregnant from the sheer amount of cum deposited into her. His satisfied balls shrunk up and then relaxed with each last spurt of ejaculate. He held nothing back. On and off for about an hour, his balls would twitch as they drizzled slightly more semen into her.

Captain Totem fell asleep on and in Rosina for the night. She fell asleep as well, satisfied in a way she had never been before. None of the cum could escape unless he withdrew. Luckily, the lab was prepared for this and had drip pans prepared underneath the females. Any sperm that dripped down would be used for artificial insemination.

Upon waking, his soggy member was surrounded by the swollen passage of the freshy taken virgin. She felt tender, but was still very well lubricated inside. His slight slippage caused a line of cum to drip out into the pan. Within minutes, Carey entered the room with a long syringe. She used it to syphon the sperm from the pan. Then, she promptly walked over to the other two girls and injected them each deeply into their fertile cunts with his sperm.

Rosina had some relief through the night when his cock had softened. But he was locked tightly inside her. His cock head's mushroom shape held his rod in her womb through the night. He finally began to awaken. The memories started to come back to him quickly, and his dick yet again grew to the monster it was. It forced her insides to become the shape of his ungodly creature. She moaned as it hardened inside her and restored in girth.

He pulled out fully, and waves of cum started to seep out of her. He plugged into her again, slapping his pouch onto her ass as he forced full stokes all the way in and out of her. He was finally able to enjoy all of her. The mess between her legs was immense. The bed held her in place as he plunged his thick cock in and out of his bitch. One more hard thrust had him arching his back inward and grabbing onto her shoulders. He came deep into her yet again. Thick white semen shot into her and warmed her insides. She knew her fate now. She was his bitch and would carry his offspring.

The next day, Carey entered the room. "I know you enjoy Rosina, but she needs to rest in another room. She is most definitely fertilized by now, but we will run some tests to be sure." Rosina limped away with Carey, leaving a cum trail. The next few weeks entailed the captain constantly pumping his load into the other two women. Their holes started to gape from his huge member. Sometimes, when he came, he would shove his dick into both of them during the same orgasm; one at a time. Their insides almost seemed to begin to shape into the form of his cock as he was inside them so often.

After some months, their bellies started to tighten and bulge out. This was a sure sign of their pregnancies. Their hanging breasts began to lactate. Their stud took great pleasure in drinking straight from them. Finally, Carey came into the room and instructed Totem to leave. He was to remain in his own bedroom, alone. But he would still be cared for and be given everything he needed to survive.

4

Experimentation

It had been seven months at the facility now. Rosina was rejoined with the other females and kept in the lab room. They all had huge bellies, and it was difficult for them to move around because of it. Carey confirmed the pregnancies with them, but would not tell them of the genders. It was kind of strange how she treated their condition. She was not excited, but rather focused. Carey herself was about 19 years old. She was very young but knew her job well. Her duties were clear, and she followed them precisely and at any cost.

The next day, Carey entered the room with syringes. They had long stems from them for deep insertion. She had three, and they were all filled with an off-white substance. It appeared to have tiny white ovular shapes in them. She instructed all the girls to get down on their knees, and they followed instructions. They felt satisfied in their pregnant state, and have not yet disagreed with any procedures there. One at a time, Carey inserted their syringes deep into their vaginas and pumped the thick fluid into them. She inserted a temporary tube behind it afterward to keep the fluid inside, and told them to keep it in the rest of the day.

After this procedure, Carey went toward the back room down the hall. "Have you injected the girls yet?" William stopped her to ask. She nodded confidently. He nodded in return and went his own way. She continued on and entered the room with the creature. It was feeding time. The room was so dark, that she couldn't see it. But this was not unusual.

She took some of the protein meal from the cabinet and began pouring it into a bowl.

A strange noise came from the enclosure. It almost sounded like a closing door. Carey looked at the enclosure, which appeared the same. She then placed the food into the flap that led into the cage. It was rare that she could get a view of the creature, despite feeding it every day. She saw the eyes reflect in the darkness again. This time, it began to walk forward. It travelled on all fours. The beast lifted its head to smell the air, but remained in the dark.

She turned away to walk toward the computer in the room. In that instant, her leg was pinned to the cage by long, black claws. The sharp talons had to be at least five inches long each. She cried out for William, but he didn't answer. The rest of the residents would surely not hear her from that distance. The creature's other hand used it's claw to easily unlock the cage gate. It's almost as though he had done it before. Carey was dragged into the cage and the door auto-locked in front of her as she was inside the cage with the creature for the first time.

Both of them were together in the darkness. He had her pinned down firmly as he sniffed over her entire body. It started to lick her here and there. Her clothes were surely in the way. The beast used its powerful jaws and tore off everything she had on. The concrete floor was incredibly cold. She almost felt bad for the creature at that moment; but it was a fleeting thought. His long, wet tongue licked over her as he became familiar with her scent and shapes.

She was then rolled onto her back. The creature had four tendrils that emerged from his jaws, but it was too dark for Carey to see this happen. All she knew was, her mouth was being pulled open from four directions. The beast's tongue emerged curiously from its throat. It was almost if it had a mind of its own. The tongue dipped into her mouth without hesitation. Then, it went into the back of her throat. It dipped into her with one stroke, and then retracted like a snake.

Two more tentacles massaged and pulled on her breasts as if to distract her from what he was doing. She couldn't help but feel turned on from the stimulation. Her body instinctively prepared itself to be bred as this was all being done to her.

His entire body had the appearance of a grotesque alien of some sort. He had both tentacles and antlers. She wondered what on earth type of experiments he could have done to himself to become this. And this entire time kept it a secret from her. Was this his plan all along?

She actually had started to have a crush on him before all this. In a twisted kind of way, she was getting what she actually longed for.

Carey coughed at the feeling of her throat being invaded. She became nervous and gasped a little. The tongue had a larger head on the end with a slit on it for an orifice. Then, it seemed to slither halfway down her esophagus. She tried to scream out. As soon as she did, the head of the tongue flared out to stop all air passageways. This prevented her from making too much noise. When the flare released, all she could do was gasp for air. She quickly learned that all she could do was obey. The tongue then stopped climbing into her, and became stiff. It started to dump a thick white fluid into her. This was a natural lubricant to prepare her for the next process. After enough was expelled down her throat, it withdrew enough to reach her mouth. Her digestive system down from her stomach to her mouth was now fully lubricated.

The tongue quickly shot back into her throat and slowed down as it got deeper inside her. It slithered until it reached her stomach. She was fully intruded by the alien-like organ. The base of the tongue had a large round object start to travel down inside it. It reached her mouth, and had to stretch out her lips to get into her mouth. It was the size of an ostrich egg. The object could clearly be seen from the outside as it travelled down her throat. It finally disappeared as it went deeper into her digestive system. At the end of its journey, a large warm sticky egg emerged from the tip of the tongue into her stomach. It had a moist film around it, and it sat heavily in her. Another one soon arrived. And, another one. Her stomach started to fill quickly. It wasn't long before the shape of the eggs could be seen through her belly. He was depositing eggs into her digestive system, and there was nothing she could do about it.

Each slimy egg forced itself past her lips as it travelled inside the invasive tongue. She instinctively swallowed each time one went down her throat, and the noise echoed against the concrete walls. She placed her one free hand on her belly. The huge eggs made her stomach look lumpy.

While the creature continued to do this, he took both of his front arms and pinned her legs apart and onto the floor. He moved his body in up close to her. His wet sheath was sopping wet with cum, even dripping down his hanging scrotum. The fleshy, wet sheath rubbed up against her pussy. His cum was fresh and warm, and it felt good to her in the cold room.

He started to rub his sheath up and down her. His hard, pointed penis began to protrude from inside the sheath as he rubbed. It explored her vertically; memorizing her hole locations. It soon found both of her openings, but didn't enter them yet. He stopped rubbing and positioned himself a certain way. The strange penis almost seemed like it was as pointed as a pencil at the end. This was how he could locate and invade any hole. It was misleading, but a necessary function to be able to breed other species. He easily slipped the sharp point into her an inch. As his cock continued to slide into her, the width increased rapidly. His cock head had a mushroom shape that had a similar diameter she would have to experience if she gave birth. His natural lubrication stretched her barriers and forced the monster inside. She orgasmed, and the beast stopped a moment to enjoy her vagina twisting and sucking on his breeding rod. Then, the cock continued its journey. It met the mouth of her womb, and he humped once to force himself into that as well. As he did this, he flares his tongue to silence her from screaming out.

The alien cock stopped there. The dick head was so far in, that it was rubbing against the far side of her womb. A trail of eggs could be seen travelling down his shaft. The size of them was like pushing his cock head into her all over again. They each plopped directly into her womb, one by one as they exited his cock head through the slit opening. A trail of slime followed each one as it dropped out.

After the third, his second pointed cock nudged itself out of his wet shaft. It prodded her ass, and located it promptly. The intruder again forced her last hole open. At this point, her expression was dazed. She was under full control of the beast. She would be forced to carry whatever offspring he had implanted into her. The eggs travelled into her ass through his secondary cock as it navigated as far as it could into her.

It began depositing eggs on the opposite side of her stomach. She was being completely filled with his huge eggs. He no longer had to hold her down. After three hours, he had filled her completely. Her throat even had large bumps where the eggs happily sat. She could hardly move. Carey was now a living incubator for his eggs.

Each of her holes were full of eggs. A large egg protruded from inside her vagina and anus. But, it was too large to come out. Her throat had a large egg resting in it as well. There was just enough room for her to breathe. The unlikely pair rested together that night. He curled around his bitch warmly.

The next day provided the creature opportunity to continue his intricate processes. His two-pointed tips peeked out from his warm sheath. They found her vaginal lips quickly, and rubbed around either side of her already gaping opening that was full of egg. The tips pressed into her from either side, inserting horizontally. Her opening stretched out and looked similar to the shape of a large eyelid. Once they entered just a couple of inches on either side of the egg, they stopped. The creature's swollen balls shrunk up into his abdomen momentarily, and the cocks spurted out cum into her with great force. Her lumpy stomach was soon smooth as it inflated with his semen. Her belly grew larger than it normally would have in a normal pregnancy at 9 months with quadruplets.

She was inseminated in every hole. A thick river of cum trickled from her each day. The special semen that was inside her was designed to keep the host alive during the process, so she didn't have to eat food. Her body absorbed the nutrients and lived on as she incubated the fertile eggs. Each night, the beast would lick her warm belly. All of her insides felt incredibly tight, but satisfying. She belonged to him   now.

5

Ongoing Oppression

Totem finally was able to enter the lab to check on his females. As he passed several rooms, he noticed a strange machine in a room. It was an artificial insemination machine.

He kept on walking. When he arrived, he found them waiting for him. Their stomachs had become severely lumpy, which was unusual for a normal pregnancy. He stayed with them, keeping them warm each night while they carried whatever was inside them. After some time, he felt the urge to breed them. However, they were so full of eggs that this was impossible. He didn't want to waste his precious sperm in their other holes, so he simply didn't mate with them during this time.

Totem cared for the female trio for weeks. Finally, something started to change. Thick, clear fluid began to slide out of Sandra. Egg cracking noises could be heard inside her.

Everyone watched silently. Totem got down and parted her vaginal lips to try to see what was going on. He saw what appeared to be large snakes writhing inside her. Her belly seemed to twirl as the snakes hatched and squirm around. They curled around her organs and enjoyed her warmth. It didn't appear that they had plans to exit her.

The other two females suffered the same fate. Snakes filled their tight bellies to the max. There was nothing any of them could do. The snakes had full control as they formed around the organs of the females and stayed there. As time passed, Totem's balls gained a weight of five pounds. It was time to breed, and he was out of his mind.

Despite the circumstances, Totem walked up to the rear of Rosina, and inserted his throbbing cock all the way into Rosina's slimy vagina. He moaned at the feeling and started to thrust rhythmically. One of the pythons noticed the new organ inside her, and didn't waste any time to wrap around it tightly. Within moments, it was wrapped so tight that he could no longer withdraw his erection. The tight serpentine clasp was enough to have him shoot all four pounds of semen into her. The snakes enjoyed the warm fluid, and seemed to gather there in it. It was also an additional source of nutrition for them. But now, he couldn't leave.

His deflated cock rested inside Rosina as he panted from the expulsion. The python was convinced it had suffocated its prey. It then wrapped its jaws around his cock head and worked its way down his shaft. The feeling was incredible to him, and he began to get another erection. Once it reached the base of his shaft, he instinctually began humping. This brought the snake's head out of Rosina, and thus the entire snake as he withdrew. The surprised python let go of

Totem's penis and hung down from her hole. It reluctantly slithered out of her and went into the room corner.

They all wondered how many snakes each girl had in them. It had to be many, with how large their bellies were. And now, Cary was missing. She was supposed to help look after them.

William walked into the room abruptly. He looked upon the three tied females, seemingly satisfied of their current state. Then, he turned his head to Totem. His spent cock and balls hung between his legs, sopping wet from the experience. "These are MY females. You were just a part of the experiment. You belong to me now."

Totem swung at him wildly with his fists. William's eyes suddenly went fully black. A guttural growl came from his throat and fangs protruded from his gums. His entire face started to disfigure as he began to transform. Totem stepped back in fear of the creature. It tore off its lab coat and grew fur in just minutes. Long claws extended from his hands and feet. Totem could not escape; the door was locked. All of the girls squirmed in their restrains, but they already knew it was to no avail.

The creature formerly known as William began to move toward Totem. In just a matter of seconds, he had Totem pinned down to the ground helplessly. The massive creature held him solidly in place. A muscular tentacle emerged and held Totem's dick firmly in an upright position. William's own phallus emerged from its fleshy sheath. It was already covered in it's own gelatin. The huge member touched heads with William's cock. Suddenly, a tendril shot out from the inside of William's alien cock. It was a very thin tentacle-like limb with a pointed tip. Totem cried out at the feeling. It shot halfway down his cock and stopped at his shriek, then hurriedly navigated deeper. The tendril slithered down, seeking it's final destination. Totem's thighs quivered at the strange intruder. What could he possibly be doing? The muscular tentacle curled around and finally nudged itself into his scrotum. The tip was all the way inside his left empty testicle.

Totem moaned outload as the girls looked on. The alien tip seemed to dance around, prodding inside his ballsack with unknown intention. The huge creature's own balls swayed as his limb explored the new territory. Totem's dick hole began to ache in pain, as the shaft of the intrusion was wider than it had ever been. At last, the creature ejaculated into his testicle. The sound of pouring liquid could be heard easily in the room. His left ball swelled up quickly. In the next moment, the limb retracted, just to enter the other testicle. It was once again filled to the brim. The creature withdrew, and left the room. Totem's sack was so heavy, he could not get up right away. The round pair laid on the cold floor, and so did he as he tried to recover.

Over the next few days, Captain Totem did all he could to expel the new contents of his balls. Despite constant ejaculation, the swelling would not go down. It was as though his body was now forced to produce the semen of another creature and reproduce that way.

6

The Cycle

Carey was struggling in her cell. Her body started to go into contractions. It was time for her to lay eggs. She got onto her hands and knees. Her huge belly rested on the floor in this position. She whined out loud, but tried to keep her volume low. She didn't want to attract her captor. The eggs had increased in size. One single egg could be seen peeking from her vaginal opening. It was white and rather large.

It became quite painful as her body attempted to expel the egg. Her hole was simply not large enough. She spread her legs to ease the pain. It seemed to be lodged in place. Warm fluid dripped down from her birthing hole. She strained to push the egg out, and it peeked out some more. As she relaxed, it sucked back into her body. It was going to take a lot of work to lay the gigantic eggs. She then parted her legs all the way; allowing all her weight to be on her pregnant belly. This immediately protruded the egg almost halfway from her vulva. She cried out in pain. Carey was sweating at this point, and used the last of her strength to push past the widest part of the egg. It slipped out of her along with a pile of seminal fluid and egg protecting fluid. The egg safely rolled to the side as she rested. Her rear was completely wet from the experience.

It took Carey a couple of weeks to lay the eggs. They were all piled up, fully incubated and soon ready to hatch. She had no idea what could possibly be inside of them. However, instinctively she protected them from harm and kept them warm as much as she could. Her breeding hole was now gaping open. After some time, it would retain its normal diameter. But she had to heal first.

It was now clear that this unique island was being used for a project unlike any other. Animal populations on earth had decreased to an alarming rate due to the wars. Meanwhile, humans have been starving of proteins typically resourced from their meats. It was a critical emergency to increase the animal and human population of the world. And now, the only safe place to do this was this island. It was up to the lone scientist the accomplish this task, in his own twisted ways.

The laboratory now had a large digital sign outside saying; "Accepting applications". The requirements said the women had to be at least 18 years of age for the experiment. They must also be of breeding age, and not already pregnant. Those applicable could apply. If they passed the application, they would be supplied ample food and water and a climate-controlled room for the duration of the experiment. They were not to ask additional questions. The women were to sign their life to the cause of aiding the animal population, but they knew not what it entailed.

The island was called Yupa. There was an unusual population on this island. Some animals roamed about, and many human females at this point. The island presented an opportunity to them. An opportunity to save the earth and repopulate the animals throughout. Even regular animals such as cows and horses had become endangered. How would this be accomplished? The advertisement did not say. But the women gathered for the cause regardless. It seemed that perhaps all of them had survived the ship crash.

On the opposite end of the island, there was a small group of past subjects on the shore of the ocean. Each were clearly pregnant. The females laid in as a comfortable position as they could. One in particular was ready to give birth. The middle-aged woman had her legs spread apart as wide as she could. A newborn foal emerged, its head and front legs protruding. It slid out of her tightly but quickly. The exhausted woman laid on the shore and watched the foal get up within minutes.

Foals seem to mature much faster than humans. The foal soon found the breasts of the lactating woman, and despite her surprise of the ordeal, she laid back and enjoyed the experience. The foal nursed the fresh milk from the woman's breasts and would continue to grow in the next few weeks and months, finally into adulthood. The woman would then be eligible to enter the project again into a cycle that would last as long as her fertility.

The laboratory would release pregnant women back onto the island periodically. They were all noticeably large and inflated in the belly region. Some of them even struggled to walk in their condition. Each one seemed to have a mystery package. While they all had very large bellies, each one appeared to have a different shape. Some carried many eggs; some carried a calf or more than one. It was a variety of young being carried. After giving birth, they cared for the young until the animals were old enough to care for themselves.

The island was able to ship adult animals to other continents upon reaching adulthood. This was the goal of the operation in order to achieve animal populations. It was a valiant task, but one needed to retain normalcy and survival in the earth. Every day, animals of many species were released into different regions. It appeared to be an effective means of repopulating the earth with animals. In turn, females were granted gratification with the feeling of being bred and giving birth. It was a natural process, however with modified steps to achieve it.

The animals on the island however, appeared to have a higher intellect than what was typical in the old world. Perhaps they had achieved a higher IQ from their mothers. In some areas, they even seemed to begin their own society. But, the ship quickly gathered their group and distributed them to different continents. Studies on these animals' intellect were not performed.

One end of the laboratory was busy with concocting injections and performing experimentations on the microscopic scale. One woman could be seen strapped to a medical bed. Her belly was extremely large. A female scientist was tending to her and performing an ultrasound. She was full of offspring. Four fawns squirmed around and kicked inside her. It felt good to her, albeit somewhat strange. The females in the lab were content with the results they had of the experiments. The feeling of being pregnant felt natural and fulfilled their instinctual needs.

7

Operation Population

After quite some time, human males were born onto the island as well. These men were kept under strict supervision, and once they reached adulthood, they were taken into the lab. Each one would go through the same process. They were to be laid down onto a table and restrained. A smooth, surgical steel grade rod was inserted into their penis and secured into place. A button would be pressed, and injected an unknown seminal fluid into the males' scrotums. Once they reached capacity and bulged just enough, they were released. It was unknown to them what the substance was. They were being injected with genetically modified animal sperm. Each woman they impregnated would be carrying young of the animal's sperm they were injected with.

The steel rod used was connected to the fluid tank that many visitors would pass by and notice. There were several compartments, with several different fluids inside. There was a complex plumbing system attached to it that appeared to come from almost every room down the hall. A label on the tank said: "Keep at 68 Degrees Fahrenheit/20 Degrees Celsius." Every day, the amount of the mysterious fluid would be different depending on how it was being used. It was tended to hourly by one of the staff. At times, a member would come in to retrieve an amount of it from the dispenser for use. The east wing was full of locked doors with hatches to view the contents of the room.

Behind the locked doors in the east wing were rooms for the test subjects. Each woman had her own room. It was kept at a comfortable temperature, and she had food and water as needed. There was a red light bulb in the top corner of the room that stayed off until it was time for the experimental procedure. When a staff member turned the button on outside the room, the woman was to get into position and get situated in the apparatus in the room. She would be secured in a specific position unique to the experiment set for her.

The west wing was a large keeping area for male subjects. It was kept clean and the men were tended to in order to keep them in pristine condition. Many varieties of experiments were done on each of the men there. Each male was kept in its own enclosure. Their door had a folder on it with paperwork with their age, species they were modified with, genetic information, and history. Staff would periodically go in and clean their stall and wash them as well. They had all the food and water they needed to thrive.

All of the staff in the lab typically handled the experiments in a very professional manner. The subjects would be cared for during the experiment, and briefed on what they can expect. They could cancel any time before the procedure, but after it began, they would have to follow through. The entire process was consensual, and the women knew they were doing it for a good cause. Even if it felt uncomfortable for a time, the end result would be helping the state of the world.

Each holding room for the women had a specially placed inset trough into the floor. The drain would catch any overflow of semen and bring it to the holding tank. None of it was to go to waste. It held mixed semen from many different species, and was well-kept so that it could be used when needed. Using this process was somewhat of a father roulette if they were given the mixed serum. Some of them were given artificial insemination, while others were given the more natural process.

The further down the wing the rooms got, the more progressed the subjects were in the experiments. Some were only allowed a specific species, others who may have appeared less fertile were given treatments from the tank. After a couple of months, their bellies would be measured. Their diameter must have grown to three times it's usual size for them to be confirmed pregnant. Until that point, they would be continuously bred daily until they met the requirements.

Changing chromosomes in an organism was all that was needed to perform interspecies impregnation. They had a high rate of success. Very few have had to be connected directly to the holding tank. One task of some the staff was to ensure the males were in place and ready, and press this button to let the females know to get into position. Our other staff take care of the other tasks.

8

Bullish

While the area was very clean, it still had a natural animal smell. The DNA alterations of the men must have also changed their scent. It smelled of hay and grain as well, because their diets would change according to the experiments. One staff member pulled out the paperwork from the folder on the wall. "Three years old, longhorn with a 96.4% fertility rate. Those are great odds." The huge bull of a man stood still, looking around wildly. His huge muscles bulged from his body. His head dipped down, as though he had horns and snorted. He had recently been injected with longhorn bull DNA. It clearly altered his mind as well.

The staff pressed a button on the wall, and another staff member approached within moments. "Check the health status of this bull and ready him." The staff member nodded and entered the stall carefully. They took a carrot from a feeding box and handed it to the male subject as a distraction. A scale the height of a stool was dragged to the rear of the bull. They carefully examined the man's testicles. He hadn't had the opportunity to breed for 3 weeks, but his time was coming. The pink and white scrotum was mostly bald, but partially furred. They almost dragged onto the ground from sheer weight. Each movement the powerful man made caused them to sway around rapidly. The staff member took both his hands and carefully cupped the balls from underneath, placing them on the scale. "Twenty-seven and a half pounds." The scientist nodded. "I'd say he's ready." The sack was picked back up and let back down to their normal resting place carefully. His huge package swayed back and forth from the momentum.

The staff member then walked to the breeder's side, and slid back the sheath just enough to view the tip of his penis. It was clear that even the physical appearance of these men was altered. It was very pointed and looked pristine. The pink spear dripped one thin line of semen onto the ground. "He has been dripping for a couple of days now. He's past due to be placed into the breeding quarters."

The staff took the large man, and walked him out of the iron-barred stall. His sheath and balls bounced and swayed with each step. He made a light trail of precum wherever he walked, in the form of small drops. Staff followed them and quickly cleaned behind him.

As they approached the mouth of the east wing, one staff leaned toward the other and told them to press the button on room 342. He went down the hallway in search of the correct number. The bullish man was brought around the rear of all of the rooms. There was a small holding room behind all the female's rooms. It was just large enough to hold a large animal. The fertile male was led into the holding room and the iron door closed behind him. He was cramped in the room, but only temporarily.

As staff reached the front of the door to room 342, they instantly pressed the button. In extreme curiosity, they opened the window slide to see what was going on. A middle-aged woman was inside, and took notice to the light. About mid-ways into the room was a device made to have her positioned in. It had two steps up into the unit. She walked up to it, and leaned forward. Her position in it had her laying down comfortably. She was tilted with her front end somewhat upward on the platform. This bed was designed specifically for bovine breeding. The bull's penis tends to jut upward; with the female positioned in this way, he would be able to obtain maximum penetration. This would be favorable for impregnation.

The woman was finely shaped, and had never become pregnant before. She got onto the platform like how she had been trained to do. A padded bar started to mechanically separate her legs apart as another one came down securely over her back. This was all that was needed to hold her into place. She waited anxiously for what was to come.

The back door containing the large bull of a man opened with the press of a button. He stood there, taking in the scent of what the room contained. His powerful arms were perhaps his most prominent feature. He entered the room very carefully, taking in his surroundings. The female lied in wait, eager and excited but also extremely nervous.

The longhorn bull-minded man could not mistake the scent of female. His pink, pointed member danced as we walked closer. It protruded only slightly from its long sheath. He finally approached the woman and his hot breath washed over her naked rear. She shuttered, then relaxed again. His long tongue licked her right buttock, leaving a thick trail of saliva on her. He licked again with his long tongue, from her belly up to her back. Her folds encapsulated around his tongue as he drew it upward.

He was now prepared to accomplish his next mission. The powerful man stood up tall, and rested his chest on the top of the bed over the woman. The momentum had his warm, heavy balls slap her stomach twice. His mission was to inject her with them. His rod was as rigid as a staff, and very pointed. It could find any small opening with ease, and slide in whatever was necessary thereafter.

His arousal soon got the better of him, and his spear began rigidly searching for its target. The pointed tip rubbed hard vertically up and down the woman's rear. She tightened up anxiously. Within just moments, he found her breeding entryway. His precum-coated tip slid in easily. He stabbed it in menacingly with short humping movements, then jumped into her. The base of his long penis had significantly more girth than the tip. It made a tight seal as he withdrew and stabbed again. Each time he stabbed, his long rod snuck into her secret entrance, deep into the far depths of her womb. She cried out, but this excited the bull-man further. His gigantic balls knocked into her rear as he vigorously used her to stimulate his long, smooth cock. He licked her neck, thanking her for the pleasure he felt.

She did not give way to his humping due to the device she was strapped to. This enabled the bull to take all the time he needed in satisfying himself. He took the lack of movement as consent and willingness to breed. He humped into her for at least half an hour. His stabs showed his pointed member protruding into her belly. Each stab poked out a bump from her as he explored her insides. Finally, each hump began to produce strands of thick, white cum. The semen flowed directly into her womb and filled her up even to the ends of her ovarian tubes. Each shot of semen felt like a shot of warm fluid into her. She felt immediately dominated by the powerful beast. Each thrust felt like a pint's worth of viable semen. After each hump, he pressed deep into her for a moment. He enjoyed the feeling of his tip poking into the far wall of her womb; with enough pressure to curl the tip and begin penetrating one of her ovarian tubes. Just this breeding alone was guaranteed to cause her to be pregnant.

She squealed with each deep thrust. His testicles tightened and twitched with each ejaculation. The longhorn bull-man's huge fleshy balls were no longer heavy. He emptied them into her, and his rod stayed buried in her for hours. Her tight stomach grew to immense proportions. The man simply stood still with his rigid member resting inside of her. Her entrance was sealed so tightly that not even a drop escaped for the duration. His hard member twitched inside of her. After some time, he released from her and his long cock hung below. The fluid all drained into the trough below, which would take it to the holding tank for future breeding of other females. The bull was taken away, and the woman was allowed to rest for the remainder of the day. Tomorrow, she would be serviced again.

The man was given ample water and supplements in order to properly and quickly facilitate sperm growth. Each day, he was taken to room 342 to service the woman for months. After each month, her belly was measured. Finally on month eight, she was able to be released onto the island. She would give birth to two healthy calves that would nurse from her up to adulthood.

9

Human Nature

Captain Totem was kept inside the laboratory. He was one of the males used in the experiments, except he was able to maintain his proper mental state for the most part. One particular female volunteer caught his eye. The second night of her stay, she was placed in her own room. Totem waited until about midnight, when he thought the entire laboratory was asleep. He snuck out from his room and sneaked over to her room. He could smell the virginity on her. Virgins were very few here and they don't last long. They were also hard to come by.

Totem was now alone in front of room 220. His member started to rise at the thought. This was his opportunity. He looked both ways around the empty hallway, then back down at the button. Then he hastily pressed the button. The light lit up in her room immediately. Without hesitation, she got into position. This room had a divider, so that she could not see the male behind her. The divider had a padded hole about mid-waist and clasped down to hold her into place.

Her legs were splayed apart by a spreader bar, and the automated mechanism clasped tightly around her ankles to hold them into place. By this time, Totem's member was throbbing immensely. He had never been this large before. It looked menacing verses her slit. He rubbed his warm tip on her rump. She quivered a bit in response. His thick head left a cum trail wherever it rubbed on her backside. There was no turning back now. He pointed his cock in an upward position and humped the underside of it against her. She tried to wiggle but the restraints kept her firmly in place. He then gripped his shaft firmly, and rubbed his wet cock hole over her openings, up and down. Captain Totem located her vaginal opening with haste. It was moist, but extremely tight. Not even a dime could fit through it. He prodded the very tip of his penis head into her impossibly tight hole. She tensed up in pain, and he withdrew it again. The action caused a suction effect. The room echoed with the noise.

He prodded her again with his veiny member. The suction felt so good. It sucked his precum directly into her breeding hole. That alone could get her pregnant. The rest was poured into the trough. His now-slimy member would be able to slip into anything. Totem started up his process again. His cock tip bounced in and out of her, creating a rhythmic suction noise. He hadn't even got it as deep as the apex of his penis head yet. The suction had at least drained him of all of his precum before he was ready to go in deeper.

His cock was dripping with animal semen from various unknown species. The female would certainly be pregnant from this session, but time will tell who the father was. He then stood firmly behind her, ensuring a straight entry. Her opening was sopping wet from his precum and animal sperm. Totem pressed his spaded head into her. It was incredibly tight. The mouth of her breeding hole squeezed his penis head firmly as he forced it in slowly. Finally, the head popped into her. It made a slick popping noise. Her virginity was now taken. The young female's breeding hole squeezed tightly around the collar of his cock head. It was the equivalent of her being knotted to him.

His penis head sealed her entryway as one shot of semen flowed into her freely. Totem tried to pull his penis out, but the pressure was immense. It was hard enough to get his head inside. Instead, he stepped up to her and in one stroke, bottomed out his veiny cock into her. She shrieked in pain and pleasure. His animal instinct suddenly took over. He gripped her hind end, and slipped his rigid dick from her just to shove it back in again fully. Within minutes he was humping into her roughly and seeping into her without control. A final pump had him in her all the way, emptying his once tight balls as they shriveled back into normal size. After emptying himself, he sat next to her and caught his breath. Breeding is a natural need and he had to fulfill it.

Before he knew it, it was morning time. Totem heard noise coming from the rear hall. He gathered himself quickly and exited the room. A staff member saw him at just the right time without compromising his situation. "Looks like you've already got her prepped for the next stallion. Thanks." Totem sighed in relief. A stallion? It was a good thing he stepped in, to help her for what was to come next. It would make the experience less painful. A handsome stallion-like man came into view.

10

Equine

The horse-like man seemed pranced in place as he was closed into the room behind the girl. He reared his muscular head and threw it about wildly. His nostrils flared out, gathering in the scent of the female who was just bred. She smelled like many other males, but this did not deter him. It was his job to become the dominant stallion.

The door opened, and he trotted out into her enclosure without hesitation. Her holding machine automatically raised her a couple feet higher up, as this man was taller than usual. Her legs and arms dangled below, with the spreader bar holding her legs firmly apart for the intruder.

The man's cock was a marbled pick and black. He had no problems keeping it in an erect position as he groomed her rump. He licked around her vigorously. Horses will signal they are not ready to breed by moving away. The girl stayed in the compromising position, ready to be taken. At this point however, she didn't have a choice. He mounted her quickly, and his large black balls swayed with each movement. His fleshy horse cock head kept flaring and unflaring in excitement. The girth of it seemed to be about as half as wide as the girl's waist. The stallion pressed it up against her. It was very warm. His tip was quite slippery with hot, thick fluid.

His blunt headed cock circled around her secret openings. This wasn't the stallion's first breeding; he knew where to go. The large surface of it felt like a hot fleshy plate rubbing across her. It pulsated with eagerness. His balls inched up into his belly for a moment, and sagged back down as precum spurted out. In that exact moment, the stallion instinctively positioned his cock hole with hers just in time to stream the hot liquid into her. She squirmed slightly at the feeling. The fertile female's rear was now covered in the stallion-man's lubricant.

This man in particular has had a tendency to be aggressive to his females. That is why the divider was made for this female. He wanted to bite on her while he entered. Instead, he was faced with a wall. This frustrated the man. He started humping with short humps, then stopping and rubbing the head against her. He knew it would be difficult to get it inside her, but the instinct to procreate was strong. He had to fill her with his foals.

Very slowly, he pressed the club shaped meat into her. His head unflared for a moment to create a more rounded spade shape for entry. This is all he needed to plunge his oversized member into her depths. The stallion nickered at the feeling. He was in her about 8 inches and had filled her to the hilt. The young girl orgasmed, and it clasped his penis even more. Her passage was now even more lubricated than before, and her insides twitched and pulsated in pleasure. He stayed in place to enjoy the feeling, then his cock head flared out inside her. It was directly up against her cervix. He bumped it into her cervix numerous times, as if to knock and ask permission to enter.

His heavy balls twitched again and tightened all the way up to his stomach, spurting another thick load into her. Then, the sack dropped back down and bounced. The female's fate was set in stone. There was no question of who was the dominant male at this point. Certainly, the offspring would be his. His humping suddenly became sharper. He put immense pressure directly into her, and the tip of his large head squeezed into her cervix one inch at a time. The stallion's muscles all became tense and his humps were strong. There was no way to stop him now. He drew back slightly. With one powerful hump, he then entered her fully. The young girl cried out and orgasmed again. His entire penis enjoyed the tightening grip of her entire vagina and this excited him further. At least a gallon's worth of highly potent sperm dumped into her womb and fertilized her immediately. He continued to stab his member into her, echoing the sound of wet suction inside the room.

He remained mounted on her for several minutes, then his thick cock fell out from her. Her orgasms had caused her body to suck in some of his semen where it would stay. The girl's womb held his semen inside it which would be used as she became pregnant.

The eager stallion-man would service her twice daily, until her belly reached proper size. After a long pregnancy, she would produce beautiful foals which would all fight to nurse from her. While the process was difficult, she was glad to have been bred and take part in repopulating the earth with animals.

11

Generations

Decades passed by quickly. The population of the island increased drastically by both man and beast. The strange thing is, William Bellows did not seem to ever age. Whatever he did during his self-experimentation may have granted him immortality. After 30 years, 85% of the island had his bloodline. Even the animal/human hybrids contained DNA from him. It was all a part of his plan, and now he was a King of the island. He also had servants, which would build a temple for him over time. William the scientist now went by the name Bakari; his God name. Everyone had to bow and obey him, as he even gained the ability to impregnate males. All of the island population was a part of his harem.

The lab was extended to be an even larger facility. One wing was dedicated just to milking. One side had mature women that were all strapped to milking machines. All of them were pregnant and producing milk for the population. The other side had their daughters. These young women were also strapped down, soon to live the same fate as their mothers. They were almost all teenagers but all of legal age; 18 and up. Each one was only about a foot apart from the next. The line contained at least 50 of the daughters.

Bakari entered the wing. Everyone turned to him in respect. He was now in his creature form. After much genetic modification, he had mastered transformation. This allowed for endless possibilities. The was the father of all of the young females. Each of them on the right side were untouched virgins. Even a human finger wouldn't be able to penetrate their hymen without severe pain and damage.

His huge claws clacked on the tile floor as he approached. Each step was a handsome display of his sex organs. His gigantic balls seemed too large for the scrotum they hung in. His wrinkly sheath hid a large secret, and the opening was moist. The entire hall went quiet. All that could be heard was the quiet hum of the milking machines draining the mothers' breasts of milk. He walked to the side that held all his daughters. The ones closer to him tried to squirm, but the restraints were too tight. He sniffed the air with his strange looking face. In one moment, he located the most fertile girl in line.

She didn't have any pubic hair, nor did any of the females. They were well taken care of by all of the staff. Bakari looked up and pressed a button above her. His daughter's legs were instantly spread apart by the machine to reveal her treasure. She was unaware of him being her father, due to her only knowing his human form. The machine spread her legs to the brink of feeling pain. It was uncomfortable, but she could tolerate it.

Bakari dropped his head down and a forked snake-like tongue flicked out. He opened his fanged jaws and let it flick into her virgin folds. She gasped at the feeling. Then, he began to lick her slit from bottom to top. She tasted like a sweet flower. His own warm tongue and saliva stimulated her easily. After thirty minutes of this, she was clearly breathing deeply and seeping of her own lubricatory fluids. Bakari's cock started to drop out of its wet sheath. It had to be almost as thick as his daughter's leg. The head was blunt, sloped thinner and then was even wider than the head at the base of the shaft. The penis head was three and a half inches wide at it's widest part. The tip seemed to have a larger slit than usual, for some reason. The base of the shaft reached 5 inches of diameter. She didn't get to view the member, as she was tied up in the opposite direction.

He then parted her vaginal opening with his huge, clawed hands. Her soon-to-be breeding hole was microscopic. Bakari took his tin tongue and flicked at the hole. Each flick was an attempt to enter her. He got her once, and she tensed up and gasped. She tasted excellent. He flicked three more times. Once more he was able to poke past her forbidden opening. He then opened his jaws wide, and forced his snake-tongue into her. The two-pronged tip ticked her insides as she tried to close her legs but couldn't. After withdrawing his tongue, she dripped her own natural juices onto the ground. The surrounding females heard what was going on and became wet instinctually from being in proximity to a breeding male.

His meaty hanging member became erect in seconds. It rubbed across her leg as he propped it onto her back. It was heavy, and half of the width of her body. He see-sawed the slimy tool slowly across her ass and back. It pulsated with every heartbeat. Each vein could be seen clearly displayed across the pink, muscular rod. Bakari stepped back to aim the brutal missile between her virgin legs. The head spurted hot cum directly onto her slit, but he was only getting started.

The cock head met her opening with gentleness. She could feel the warmth from it. It was well-lubricated so there was no friction as it moved around a little. He took his rigid member in his hand, and moved it side to side. This parted her vaginal lips as his tip kissed her opening. This is what she was born to do. She would be a breeder the rest of her life, just like the rest of them. Bakari's cock appeared to have a mind of its own as it pulsated. He stepped forward and applied pressure. Her warm hymen wall wouldn't give up her virginity easily. Especially for a cock of his size. His thirty-inch-long penis curved as he tried to push it inside her. She moaned in pain. After many years of breeding, his patience had started to wane.

He stepped back, and repositioned himself. His slitted cock was placed back up against her opening. He grabbed her breasts and leaned over her body, putting much of his weight on her. It was a reminder of who she belonged to. She whimpered as she had less air and thus could struggle less. One clawed hand went around her mouth to suppress the noise he suspected she was about to make. He pressed the offender into her again, this time with much more force. It started out crooked, and then popped into her canal tightly halfway. Fifteen inches of cock was now shoved directly into her womb. She cried out in pain, but the noise was muffled. He stepped further in and continued to shove all thirty inches into her. The head of his dick shape could be seen bulging into her throat. He no longer had to hold her mouth closed, as the cock silenced her noise as it entered her esophagus.

He fucked her to the hilt. Her hole was suddenly being forced open at a five-inch diameter. The process was necessary though, and the impregnations were for the good of the island. Each time he shoved it all the way into her, she tried to cry out but was cut short in silence as it entered her throat. Each thrust entered her all of the way. His gigantic balls hit her ass each time. They seemed to be strangely hard and tight.

He pumped into her for quite some time. Finally, was the time to give her offspring. He withdrew halfway, so that the cock head was aimed directly into her womb. But then, something strange happened. His balls twitched and twisted. One testicle appeared to move upward. It migrated from the sack and travelled into the base of his cock. It was an egg. At eight inches diameter, inserting it would be no easy task. His penis muscles pushed it further in, as the shape finally reached her opening. She was already so tight. Bakari took his hand and squeezed behind the egg, forcing it into her. This time she was allowed to cry out.

She gasped for air as the apex of the egg was forced into her. Finally, it dropped into her womb. It could clearly be seen as it fell down and dropped safely into her belly. The second egg was slightly larger, but no task Bakari couldn't handle. When it reached her opening again, he humped sharply into her, which allowed it to pop in and meet the other egg. He sprayed seminal fluid into her, and his soggy cock fell out of her. Her defiled opening was gaping now. Bakari was proud of this breeding session. He would go on to breed thousands more.

Carey was kept in her cage for the rest of her fertile years for repopulation purposes.

After much genetic modification, he was able to ensure that no negative qualities would result from inbreeding. For generations, he was worshipped as the sex God that he was. The population continued to build temples in his name and worshipped him for endless generations thereafter.

www.ingramcontent.com/pod-product-compliance
Lightning Source LLC
Chambersburg PA
CBHW071602180626
46817CB00013B/2056